Alien
Adventures

Chamber of
Treasures

Karen Ball • Jonatronix

OXFORD

Max's mission log

We are travelling through space on board the micro-ship Excelsa with our new friends, Nok and Seven.

We're on a mission to save Planet Exis (Nok's home planet), which is running out of power. We need to collect four fragments that have been hidden throughout the Beta-Prime Galaxy. Together the fragments form the Core of Exis. Only the Core will restore power to the planet.

It's not easy. A space villain called Badlaw wants the power of the Core for himself. His army of robotic Krools is never far behind us!

Fragments collected so far: 1

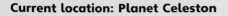

In our last adventure ...

Cat and I made our way through the maze of passages inside the Crystal Pyramid looking for Nok.

The pyramid was full of traps! At one point we were nearly squashed by a ball covered in ruby spikes!

Ant and Tiger had also made it inside the pyramid and were chased by Krool 1. At last we were reunited outside a huge chamber. Inside, we saw Nok trapped in a cage.

Max, Cat, Ant and Tiger crept into the chamber and hid behind a pile of crystals. They gasped as they looked around. Hanging from the ceiling were ruby cages filled with treasures.

They could see Nok trapped inside
one of the cages.

Two Minatrolls stood guard below. A
pair of pyrite panthers sat at their feet.

"How are we going to rescue Nok?" whispered Cat.

"I don't know," said Max. "Let's take a closer look round the chamber." The friends pressed their buttons and shrank.

Just then, the Minatrolls spun round. The micro-friends froze.

"They've seen us!" hissed Ant.

To the friends' surprise, the Minatrolls looked straight past them.

Standing in the entrance to the chamber was Krool 1. He was staring at Nok.

Chapter 2 – Attack!

"Give me that prisoner!" Krool 1 shouted. His metallic voice echoed around the chamber.

"Attack!" shrieked one of the Minatrolls.

The Minatroll shot red rays at Krool 1. Krool 1 fired an energy ball back.

A ray smashed into Krool 1's chest and sent him tumbling back into the passage.

"After him!" ordered the other Minatroll.

The panthers and the Minatrolls raced after Krool 1.

The friends were left alone in the chamber. They quickly grew back to normal size.

They peered at the cages above them. "Help!" cried Nok.

"Don't worry," Tiger shouted. "We'll fly up and break you out."

"No, you can't!" shouted Nok. "The cages are alarmed."

Chapter 3 – Free at last

"What can we do, Nok?" asked Max.

"The controls to the cages are in those huge pillars," Nok said. "Different pillars control different cages."

Before Nok could say any more, Tiger ran over to the nearest pillar.

Tiger opened a door in the pillar. He found a handle inside and began to turn it. There was a grinding noise. One of the cages started to lower down ... but not the one with Nok inside.

Frustrated, Tiger let go of the handle. It whizzed round and round. The cage hit the ground with a *THUNK!* The door burst open and jewels scattered everywhere.

"Be careful, Tiger!" hissed Cat.

Ant ran to another pillar. He opened the door, turned the handle ... and Nok's cage started to sink.

As soon as the cage touched the ground, Nok shoved the door open. He ran out to greet his friends.

As Tiger took a step forward, he felt something under his boot. He looked down and gasped. "The fragment!"

Nok grinned. "Well done, Tiger!"

Cat smiled. "We should get out of here before the Minatrolls get back."

Chapter 4 – A helping hand

The children hurried out of the chamber. They had not gone far when they heard a soft padding noise.

Suddenly, a pyrite panther leapt out in front of them. To the children's surprise, it began to purr!

The panther turned and bounded off down a passage.

"It's the panther we rescued, Cat," Max said. Max and Cat had helped the big cat when it was trapped. "I think it wants us to follow it."

They ran after the panther through the maze of passageways.

Finally, they reached a door. The panther leant on the wall and the door slid open.

There was no sign of the Krools.

"Where have they gone?" asked Cat.

"Who cares?" said Tiger. "Let's get out of here!"

The panther started to cross the moat. Tiger and Ant looked nervously at the bubbling liquid.

"Follow the panther. It knows the way," Max said.

The friends copied the panther's route. They jumped safely from one stepping stone to the next.

Chapter 5 – Outnumbered!

Just as they jumped clear of the moat, they heard a rumbling sound.

From behind the pyramid appeared an army of Badlaw's green robots. The friends were outnumbered!

The Krools uncurled themselves and moved forwards. They were ready to attack.

The panther snarled at the Krools, but the Krools kept on coming.

Just then, the two Minatrolls came pounding out of the pyramid. They were chasing Krool 1. More Minatrolls appeared from behind the crystal rocks.

"Attack!" commanded Krool 1.

The Krools launched a ferocious attack on the Minatrolls. The Minatrolls shot back with their deadly rays.

"We need to get away," said Max.

They pressed their buttons. As they shrank, the friends began to fade.

"Welcome back," said Seven. He had teleported them back to the ship.

Nok slotted the fragment into its storage box. "We did it!" he said.

"Only two fragments to go," Tiger said. "Let's hope the others are easier to find!"

Find out what happens next in *Swamp Crash*.